BROTHER ANANSI
AND THE CATTLE RANCH
– – –
EL HERMANO ANANSI
Y EL RANCHO DE GANADO

Told by / Contado por
JAMES DE SAUZA
Adapted by / Adaptado por
HARRIET ROHMER
Illustrations by / Ilustraciones por
STEPHEN VON MASON
Version in Spanish / Versión en español
ROSALMA ZUBIZARRETA

CHILDREN'S BOOK PRESS · SAN FRANCISCO & EMERYVILLE, CALIFORNIA

Spanish language consultant: Dr. Alma Flor Ada
Design: Seventeenth Street Studios.
Typesetting: Another Point
Photography: Lee Fatherree
Printed in Hong Kong through Interprint, San Francisco.

Children's Book Press is a nonprofit community publisher.

Library of Congress Cataloging-in-Publication Data

De Sauza, James.
   Brother Anansi and the cattle ranch / told by James de Sauza: adapted by Harriet Rohmer; illustrations by Stephen Von Mason: version in Spanish, Rosalma Zubizaretta & Alma Flor Ada / El hermano Anansi y el rancho de ganado / contado por James de Sauza: adaptado por Harriet Rohmer; illustraciones por Stephen Von Mason; versión en español, Rosalma Zubizarreta y Alma Flor Ada.
   Summary: A bilingual folk tale in which Brother Anansi persuades Brother Tiger to go into the cattle-raising business.
   ISBN 0-89239-044-1:
   1. Anansi (Legendary character)—Juvenile literature. [1. Anansi (Legendary character) 2. Folklore 3. Spanish language materials—Bilingual.] I. Rohmer, Harriet. II. Von Mason, Stephen, ill. III. Title. IV. Title: Hermano Anansi y el rancho de ganado.
   PZ74.1.D4 1989   398.2′452544—do19   88-37091   CIP   AC

For the children of the Atlantic Coast of Nicaragua
Para los niños de la Costa Atlantica de Nicaragua
James de Sauza

For the children of Oakland, California
Para los niños de Oakland, California
Stephen Von Mason

I'd like to thank Lorrie A. Bordelon for her
understanding and support.
S.V.M.

Brother Anansi, the spider, is a folk hero from the Ashanti people of West Africa. He also lives in the Caribbean, in Central America, and in North America—wherever African-American people tell his stories. Sometimes he is a man; sometimes he is a spider. Sometimes he is good; sometimes he is bad. But he is always very, very tricky.

El hermano Anansi, la araña, es un héroe folklórico de la tribu Ashanti del África Occidental. También vive en el Caribe, en América Central, y en Norteamérica—en todos los lugares donde las gentes afroamericanas cuentan sus cuentos. Algunas veces es un hombre; otras veces es una araña. Algunas veces es bueno; otras veces es malo. Pero siempre es muy, muy pícaro.

5

One day Brother Anansi heard that Brother Tiger won the lottery. So Anansi said to himself, "Hmmm, well now's my chance to get in Brother Tiger's pocket."

"We got some money now, eh Brother Tiger?" said Anansi.

And Tiger answered, "Well, yes, boy. I won half a million!"

Un día, el hermano Anansi oyó que el hermano Tigre se había ganado la lotería. Anansi se dijo a si mismo: —Uy, aquí está mi oportunidad de meterme en el bolsillo del hermano Tigre.

—¿Así que tenemos dinero ahora, Hermano Tigre? —dijo Anansi.

Y Tigre contestó: —Pues sí, chico. ¡Gané medio millón!

You know what?" said Brother Anansi. "I think we'd better go in for cattle raising. I have a nice green pasture all prepared with a nice little river running right through the middle. So I'm going to get the place in order and you go get the cattle."

"That's a good idea, Brother Anansi," said Tiger. "We could sell meat, milk and cheese. We could ship to the United States and South America. We could make big business."

Sabes qué? —dijo el hermano Anansi—. Creo que debiéramos empezar a criar ganado. Tengo un prado verde ya listo con un bonito riachuelo que lo atraviesa justo por la mitad. Así que voy a ir a arreglar el lugar, y tú anda a conseguir el ganado.

—Es buena idea, Hermano Anansi —dijo Tigre—. Podríamos vender carne, leche y queso. Podríamos exportar a los Estados Unidos y a Suramérica. Podríamos hacer un gran negocio.

Good. They got ready. Brother Tiger took all the money he won in the lottery and went and bought the cattle. Then they made a bridge across the river. Brother Anansi brought his family to live on one side of the river and Tiger and his family lived on the other side. They got workmen and soon everything was going pretty.

Bueno. Se prepararon. El hermano Tigre tomó todo el dinero que se había ganado en la lotería y fue y compró ganado. Luego construyeron un puente que cruzaba el río. El hermano Anansi trajo a su familia a vivir a un lado del río. Tigre y su familia vivían al otro lado. Consiguieron trabajadores y pronto todo estaba en marcha.

After a few years they had a lot of animals and business was booming. So Brother Anansi figured, "This is long enough. I think I better put it over on Brother Tiger and go about my business."

Después de unos cuantos años, tenían muchos animales y el negocio estaba yendo muy bien. Entonces el hermano Anansi decidió: —Ya ha pasado suficiente tiempo. Es hora que le haga el juego al hermano Tigre, y siga mi propio rumbo.

Brother Tiger, you know what?" said Anansi. "Now that my children are big and yours too, I think that I should take care of my own and you take care of yours. The best thing for us is to share the animals."

"Alright, Anansi, just what you say," answered Brother Tiger.

Hermano Tigre, ¿sabes qué? —dijo Anansi—. Ahora que mis hijos han crecido y los tuyos también, creo que yo debería cuidar de los míos y tú de los tuyos. Lo mejor sería repartir los animales.

—Muy bien, Anansi, como quieras —contestó el hermano Tigre.

The next day Anansi came over very late in the day. He knew that night would catch them before he could drive his animals over the bridge. After they had counted all the animals Brother Anansi said, "Now we're going to pick. You take one and I take one. You take one and I take one."

Al siguiente día Anansi vino cuando ya era muy tarde. Él sabía que iba a oscurecer antes que pudiera arrear a sus animales al otro lado del puente. Después que habían contado todos los animales el hermano Anansi dijo: —Ahora vamos a escoger. Escoge uno tú, y otro yo. Uno tú, y otro yo.

Well, they picked like that until they finished with all the animals. Then Brother Anansi said, "You know what, Brother Tiger? It's too late so I won't be able to drive my animals over. The best thing to do is to mark them. Then I'll come back."

"Okay, Anansi," said Brother Tiger. "But how are we going to mark them?"

"You leave that to me, man," said Anansi.

Siguieron escogiendo de ese modo hasta que se repartieron todos los animales. Luego el hermano Anansi dijo: —¿Sabes qué, Hermano Tigre? Es demasiado tarde para arrear a mis animales al otro lado del puente. Lo mejor sería marcarlos, y luego regresaré por ellos.

—Muy bien, Anansi —dijo el hermano Tigre—. Pero, ¿cómo los vamos a marcar?

—No tengas cuidado, hombre —dijo Anansi.

Now Brother Anansi was carrying a whole pack of pins and there was an olive tree right there where they were sharing the animals.

"I'm going to put green leaves on the ears of your animals and dry leaves on the ears of my animals," said Anansi. "Then tomorrow when I come back we will know that all the animals that have on dry leaves are mine and all the ones with green leaves are yours."

"Good," said Tiger. And they put the leaves on the animals.

El hermano Anansi traía consigo un paquete entero de alfileres. Un olivo crecía muy cerca de donde estaban repartiendo los animales.

—Voy a prenderle a tus animales hojas verdes en las orejas. Y a los míos, ojas secas —dijo Anansi—. Luego mañana cuando regrese, sabremos que todos los animales que tienen hojas secas son los míos y todos los que tienen hojas verdes son los tuyos.

—Bien —dijo Tigre. Y les prendieron las hojas a los animales.

Then Brother Anansi hid from Brother Tiger for a whole week.

"Where is that Brother Anansi?" wondered Tiger.

But Brother Anansi didn't come back until he figured all the leaves were dry.

Luego el hermano Anansi se escondió del hermano Tigre por una semana entera.

—¿A dónde se habrá metido ese hermano Anansi? —se preguntaba Tigre.

Pero Anansi no regresó hasta que pensó que todas las hojas ya se habrían secado.

When Brother Anansi finally came back, Brother Tiger said, "Okay, Anansi. I waited long enough. Now you're here and we're going to share the animals."

But Brother Anansi didn't answer. He just started to call up all the animals. Every one of them had on dry leaves.

Then Brother Anansi began to tell the animals: "Shoo, go! You there for me! Shoo, go! You there for me!"

Cuando el hermano Anansi por fin regresó, el hermano Tigre le dijo: —Bueno, Anansi. Te esperé bastante tiempo. Ahora que estás aquí, vamos a repartir los animales.

Pero el hermano Anansi no le contestó. Simplemente comenzó a llamar a todos los animales. Cada uno de ellos tenía prendido una hoja seca.

Entonces el hermano Anansi comenzó a decirle a los animales: —¡Oye tú, ándale! ¡Eres mío! ¡Oye tú, ándale! ¡Eres mío!

Brother Anansi stayed there and drove over all the animals to his side of the bridge. When the last one came, a big man cow, he looked at it and thought it was too bad that Tiger got none of the animals. So he said:

"You know, Brother Tiger, you better take this one. I think this one is for you."

El hermano Anansi se quedó allí y arreó a todos los animales a su lado del puente. Cuando vino el último, un gran buey, Anansi lo miró y pensó que era una pena que Tigre se quedase sin ningún animal. Así que dijo:

—Sabes, Hermano Tigre, mejor te quedas con éste. Creo que éste es tuyo.

So Brother Tiger was left with just one big man cow. At the end of the story Tiger was left broke and Anansi had gotten rich.

"You put it over on me this time, man," said Brother Tiger. "But next time, Brother Anansi, I'm going to get even. You just wait!"

Así que el hermano Tigre se quedó con sólo un gran buey. Al final del cuento, Tigre acabó pobre y Anansi se había vuelto rico.

—Me la ganaste esta vez, hombre —dijo el hermano Tigre—. Pero la próxima vez, Hermano Anansi, me voy a desquitar. ¡Espérate nomás!

About the Story

The stories of Brother Anansi the Spider were brought by African people to the Americas. From Jamaica, the Anansi stories came to the Atlantic Coast of Nicaragua where in African-American towns like Bluefields and Pearl Lagoon, the traditional tales have thrived and acquired new and contemporary dimensions.

Brother Anansi and the Cattle Ranch was told to me by James de Sauza, a carpenter, fisherman and church leader from Pearl Lagoon, Nicaragua. In Pearl Lagoon, the oral tradition is still very much alive, so de Sauza's tale touches on modern themes, such as cattle ranching and the lottery. He tells his stories in a version of Creole English, the language of the people, which has African roots. I have retained his language, making only a few changes, many of them suggested by Miss Adela Savery, a retired high school teacher from Bluefields, Nicaragua, who has a profound knowledge of both Creole and Standard English.

The pictures are by Stephen Von Mason, a brilliant young African-American painter and printmaker from Oakland, California. In keeping with the authentic tone of the story, Von Mason has portrayed Brother Tiger as a jaguar. There are no tigers in Central America, but jaguars are powerful and revered animals and are referred to as tigers in the folklore of the area. Von Mason has used acrylic paints and colored pencils on rag paper for this, his first picture book for young people.

My thanks go go Bishop John Wilson, Ray Hooker, Rev. Joe Kelly, Miss Adela Savery, Carlos Rigby, Alice Slade, Ronald Brooks, Robert Brooks, Bea Julian, David Schecter and the teachers of Bluefields, Pearl Lagoon and Corn Island for their help on this project.

Harriet Rohmer
San Francisco, California

32